THE DARE

THE DARE

John Boyne

BBC
LARGE
PRINT

First published in 2009 by
Transworld Publishers
This Large Print edition published
2009 by BBC Audiobooks by
arrangement with
Transworld Publishers

ISBN 978 1 4056 2259 2

British Library Cataloguing in Publication Data available

Printed and bound in Great Britain by
CPI Antony Rowe, Chippenham and Eastbourne

CHAPTER ONE

It started on a Wednesday evening in July, a few days after my school holidays began.

I'd spent the afternoon playing football with Luke Kennedy. He lived with his mam and her boyfriend in the house next to ours. His dad didn't live there any more. He'd moved out two years before, the day after Luke's tenth birthday. He brought him to see Norwich play Arsenal that weekend to make up for it. Norwich lost.

No one was in when I got home, which was strange. It was only half past four so I knew Dad wouldn't be home for another hour yet, but Mam wasn't usually out at this time of the day. I went in to the kitchen, opened the fridge and drank some milk straight from the carton. I liked being home alone, although it was better if it was closer to Christmas and I could look for hidden presents. There wasn't that much to do during the summer.

I went upstairs and stopped outside Pete's room. He'd been at university since October and was supposed to be coming back for the summer to work in Dad's shop, but he'd phoned a few days earlier to say that he was going to take a train around Europe with his friends instead.

'Bloody typical,' Dad said after the call. 'He makes a promise and then breaks it.'

'He's young,' said Mam. 'Can you blame him?' She always stuck up for Pete because he was her favourite. Everyone said he looked like a movie star and that he could charm the pants off an elephant.

'You're not to mind,' Gran told me once. 'You have the brains in the family and looks aren't everything anyway.'

That made me feel great.

Pete took most of his things to university with him—all the good stuff anyway. When he went, I hoped that he'd leave his stereo behind because it was better than mine, but he didn't. He took most of his CDs too and left the rubbish ones in a pile by the door. His wardrobe was mostly empty. The hangers inside reminded me of skeletons.

He had a box at the top of the wardrobe filled with things that he wanted to keep but hadn't taken with him. It was sealed with masking tape, and I opened it once when no one was around to look at the magazines he kept there. The next day I bought some masking tape of my own so that I could open the box and look at them whenever I wanted. Then I could seal it again and no one would ever know.

I sat down on the bed and wished he was there to talk to. Pete wasn't like the other big brothers I knew, the ones who were still in school. They always ignored their little brothers when they saw them, but Pete never did that.

I went back to my room and looked out of the window. Luke Kennedy was talking to himself as he knelt beside his bike, checking the back wheel for punctures. I didn't want him to see me so I knelt down under the windowsill and kept watching until he went back indoors.

I didn't start to think anything was wrong for a while.

'There you are,' said Dad when he came home. By now I was stretched out on the sofa, watching television. 'How was your day?'

'Fine,' I said. 'I went cycling with Luke. Then we played football.'

'They should take all bikes off the road,' he said, shaking his head. 'They're a menace.'

'Maybe they should take all the cars off the road instead,' I said. 'And make everyone ride bikes. There's too much pollution, if you ask me.' There was a story on the news about pollution right at that moment. That's why I mentioned it.

'Brilliant, Danny,' said Dad, patting me on the head as if I was a dog. 'That's the solution.' I didn't say anything. Dad always thought he was being funny when he was being sarcastic. 'Where's your mother?' he asked finally, looking around. He seemed surprised that she wasn't standing there with his slippers and a cup of tea.

'She wasn't here when I got home,' I said.

'What time was that?'

'Half past four.'

'That's odd,' he said, glancing at his watch. 'And she didn't phone to say she was going out?'

'No.'

'Or leave you a note?'

'I didn't see a note,' I said after a moment. 'But I didn't really look either.'

Normally, if she wasn't going to be home on time, Mam left a message on the pad by the phone. I'd forgotten to look when I got home. Dad went in to the hall and came back a moment later, shaking his head.

'No note,' he said. 'She must be held up somewhere. Are you hungry?'

I thought about it. 'I'm starving,' I said.

*   *   *

By eight o'clock, Mam still wasn't home and Dad was starting to get worried. He phoned a few of her friends but they hadn't heard from her either. I knew he wanted to phone some more people, but this had happened once before and there'd been trouble. It turned out that Mam had met someone she knew at the library and they'd gone for a drink together and ended up staying out longer than they'd intended.

'Can I not have a life of my own?' she asked when she heard about his phone calls. 'Or do I have to clear my plans with you first?'

'No,' said Dad, smiling at her as he answered the first question. 'And yes.'

He thought he was being funny again. She hardly spoke to him for days after that, and Pete and I had to make the dinners because Dad claimed he couldn't even boil water without burning it.

'You better go to bed,' he said at half past nine when she still hadn't come home.

'But I'm on holidays,' I said. 'I've no school in the morning.'

'You still need your sleep,' he said. 'So just do as you're told, please, young man.'

Normally I would have tried to hold out for a bit longer, but I could see that he was worried. I was starting to worry too and thought I might be better off worrying alone in my bedroom than down there with him. So I went upstairs and put a CD on, but after a few seconds I turned it off because I didn't want to miss the sound of Mam putting her key in the door downstairs.

I went over to the bedroom window and looked out. Mrs Kennedy's window was facing mine and sometimes I saw her in her room when I went to pull my curtains before going to bed. Once I saw her in her bra and I went bright red, even though I was alone in the room. She didn't notice me standing there watching her but when I pulled the curtains, I thought I saw her turn her head. After that I wasn't able to look her in the eye for months.

I put my pyjamas on and stared down at my feet, trying to move each toe one at a time without moving any of the other ones, but I couldn't do it.

I'd started to read *David Copperfield* by Charles Dickens but, when I tried to get back to it now, I couldn't concentrate and kept reading the same line over and over again.

And then I heard the sound of a car coming down the driveway but it didn't sound like Mam's car. Hers was a little runaround and she called it Bertha, which always made me laugh. Although once, when I was in a bad mood, I told her I thought it was stupid to give a car a name and she told me that I shouldn't take everything so seriously, that it was only a bit of fun. At first I thought the car was driving past the house but then I heard it stop and the engine turned off, the doors opened and slammed shut again.

I went to my door and opened it, stepping across to the top of the stairs where I could see down to the hallway, standing where no one could see me. The bell rang and Dad came out, walked quickly towards the door and opened it. Mam was standing outside, not looking up at him but not looking at the ground either. It was like she'd focused on a spot on the wall behind him and was just going to keep staring at it for ever.

On either side of her was a policeman. But one of them took her hat off and a lot of blonde hair fell around her shoulders and I realized that one was a policewoman. Everyone looked very serious.

It didn't take a genius to figure out that something bad had happened.

CHAPTER TWO

'Rachel,' said Dad, looking at each of them in turn.

'Mr Delaney,' said the policeman. 'Could we come inside please?'

Dad nodded and stepped out of the way as they came in to the hall.

'What's happened?' asked Dad, closing the door. I was kneeling with my face at the banister now, trying to remain very quiet so no one would hear me. 'Has there been an accident? Did something happen to your car?'

The police looked at each other and then towards Mam, who didn't really seem like Mam at all.

'Would somebody please tell me what's going on?' insisted Dad after a moment. 'Constable?'

'You'll confirm that this lady is your wife, Mr Delaney?' he asked and he took his helmet off now too.

His head was shaved and he didn't look much older than Pete, which made me feel better. The policewoman looked like the lady off *Property Ladder*.

'Yes, of course she's my wife,' said Dad angrily. 'Rachel, what's all this about? Would somebody please just—'

'If you could calm down for a moment please, sir,' said the policeman. 'We'll explain it all to you then.'

'Calm down? My wife goes missing for hours on end and then she comes home in a police car and you want me to calm down? Where's she been? What's happened?' Dad demanded.

'Perhaps we could sit down somewhere,' the policewoman said. 'Your wife has had a shock and a nice cup of tea might do her the world of good right now.'

'Fine,' said Dad. 'Let's go in to the kitchen and I'll put the kettle on. But

I want to know what's happened then. Is that understood?'

'Of course, sir,' she said and they disappeared out of sight and I couldn't hear them any more, except for the young policeman. He stayed in the hall and put his helmet on the floor before looking at himself in the mirror. He turned his head left, then right, and pulled down his jacket to straighten out the creases. When he turned around he looked up and saw me. I wanted to run away but he just sort of smiled sadly at me and shook his head before following the others in to the kitchen.

It was now that I started to feel worried about Pete. He hadn't phoned us in a couple of days, not since he'd said he was going travelling, and wasn't going to be stuck in Dad's shop for three months while his friends were off having a good time. Mam had said at breakfast that if he hadn't phoned by the time *Coronation Street* was over, she was going to call him.

'I don't know why you bother,' Dad had said. 'Ungrateful little pup.'

Maybe something had happened to him, and the police had come to tell Mam and she'd gone to the station with them and he was there and he was in trouble. Or worse. Something bad had happened to Pete and I hadn't even spoken to him on the phone the other night, because everyone was fighting so much that they hadn't let me.

I made my way down the steps quietly but I still couldn't hear the voices very well. The policeman's helmet was on the floor next to the telephone stand. I picked it up and stared at it.

It was one of those old-fashioned constable's hats, solid and tall, with a Norfolk Police emblem on the front of it. It was quite heavy and when I put it on, I felt like I was being crowned King. It was far too big for me and came down to just over my

14

eyes and I didn't know how he could wear it all day.

The kitchen door opened then and I spun around to see Dad, whose face looked even redder now than before, leading the policeman and woman back in to the hallway. The three of them stopped and stared at me, and I got embarrassed because I was only wearing my pyjamas and the policeman's helmet.

'I'm sorry, Constable,' said Dad, taking it off me. 'Danny, go up to your room right now.'

I shot up the stairs and closed my bedroom door with me still on the outside before going back to my position at the banister.

Dad opened the front door then and the police stepped outside.

'If there's any news,' began Dad, but the policewoman cut him off. She had a very serious voice.

'We'll be in touch immediately, of course,' she said. 'But we will need to speak to her again tomorrow. You do understand that?'

'Of course,' said Dad. 'It's a terrible thing.'

'It's procedure, Mr Delaney,' said the policewoman. 'We'll speak to you soon.'

I heard them walk away then and Dad closed the front door but didn't move for a moment. I could see him standing there, staring at the wall, and running his hand across his eyes as he sighed. Then he went back in to the kitchen and closed the door behind him and everything went very quiet.

*   *   *

After Mam went to bed, Dad came upstairs to talk to me. I was lying down but sat up when he came into my room.

'You're still awake,' he said.

'I couldn't sleep. What's happened? Is Pete all right?'

'Pete?' he asked. 'Yes, he's fine.

Oh, I suppose I better call him too. Well, tomorrow. It'll keep until then.'

'What happened?' I asked, sitting up.

'An accident,' he said then in a gentle voice. 'Now you're not to get too upset. A little boy, he ran out in front of your mother. In front of your mother's car, I mean. He just ran out of nowhere, you see. It wasn't anyone's fault.'

I stared. I didn't know what to say. My eyes blinked a few times and I waited for him to continue.

'Now he's all right,' he said. 'Well, he's in a bad way, actually, but he's in the hospital which is the best place for him, of course. He'll be getting the best treatment there and he'll be fine, I'm sure of it.'

'How can you be sure of it?' I asked.

'Because he has to be,' he said firmly. 'You're not to worry, do you hear me? Everything's going to be fine. Just get some sleep and in the

17

morning try to stay quiet and don't bother your mother. She's very upset.'

I nodded and he left the room and went down the corridor, but I didn't lie down until I heard his bedroom door close. Then I closed my eyes and thought of the little boy and hoped that he was all right, but something told me that he wasn't going to be and that nothing was going to be the same at home ever again.

CHAPTER THREE

The next morning I woke up early. When I came downstairs Dad was already in the kitchen but there was no sign of Mam.

'She's going to stay in bed this morning,' he told me. 'She hardly got any sleep last night at all. Just stay out of the way if you can.'

I did stay out of the way, but mostly because I was afraid of seeing her. I didn't know what I'd say if I did. But later in the morning, when I went upstairs to get *David Copperfield*, she came out of the bathroom and when she saw me she burst into tears.

'For pity's sake, Danny,' said Dad, running up the stairs. 'I asked you not to cause any trouble.'

'I didn't,' I said, holding my book in the air. 'I only came upstairs for this.'

'Just go outside,' he said, shaking his head. 'Honestly, you never listen, do you?'

I went in to the garden and sat on the swing, trying to read my book, but I was getting nowhere with it. I was too angry to concentrate so I went out on my bike instead.

When I got home that night the house was empty again. It was almost six o'clock and I was hungry. I opened the fridge and thought about making a sandwich, but before I could there was a knock on the front door.

'Danny?' called a woman's voice. 'Danny, it's Alice Kennedy. Are you in there?'

I walked down the hallway and opened the door, but not all the way, and poked my head around it, like the old women do in the ads on television when the gas man comes to read the meter. Only he isn't the gas man at all, he's come to steal their pension money and beat them up. 'Hello,' I said.

'Hi, Danny,' she said, smiling.

'Mam's not home,' I said, because when women came around to the house it was always to see Mam.

'I know she's not,' said Mrs Kennedy. 'Your dad phoned me. He thought you might be hungry.'

'Well I didn't have any lunch,' I admitted.

'And here it is getting on for six o'clock,' she said, reaching a hand out through the gap between us. 'We thought maybe you should come over to ours for some dinner.'

'Mam might be making dinner later,' I said quietly, looking down at my shoes.

'Your dad said they'd get themselves something on the way home. He asked if I'd let you eat with us and I said of course,' she said. 'We'd be delighted with the company. Luke's setting another place even as I speak. But you better come with me now because I don't want the steaks to burn.'

She practically dragged me from the house and I pulled the door shut behind me. It felt nice having her hold my hand. Her skin was soft and her hand was nearly as small as my own. But I didn't want Luke to see me walking through the door hand in hand with his mam, so I pulled mine loose before we went inside.

'They call this summer,' she said as we walked along, smiling at me as if neither of us had a care in the world. As if nothing bad was happening in my house and Mr Kennedy was still living in hers. 'It's not like the summers we had when I was a girl, I can tell you that. There was a bit of heat in the sun back then.'

Inside, I could smell the meat cooking beneath the grill.

'We're back,' she said cheerfully as we stepped in to the kitchen. I looked around and could see Luke sitting at the table, staring at me as if he wasn't sure why I was there at all.

Benjamin Benson, Mrs Kennedy's boyfriend, was standing by the cooker, stirring a pot, and he turned to smile at me. He was the biggest man I'd ever seen in my life. Practically a giant, with thick, snowy white hair and a bushy white beard. I always thought he looked like a polar bear.

'Good evening, young Danny,' said Mr Benson, who spoke like someone from a different century. 'Luckily, I bought an extra steak just in case we had company. Always be prepared, that's my motto. Were you ever a Boy Scout?'

'No,' I said.

'Boy Scouts are gay,' said Luke, and Mr Benson turned to look at him and nodded.

'I dare say some of them are,' he said. 'And some are sad, and some excitable, and some delirious. We're all prone to different natures. I hope you like mushroom sauce, Danny.'

'I love it,' I said.

'Excellent,' he cried, returning to his pot and stirring it some more. He lifted the wooden spoon and held it towards me. 'Taste this and tell me whether it needs more salt. Remember, you can always add but you can never take away. Unlike a haircut. There you can always take more away but you can never put any back on.'

I pressed my lips carefully to the tip of the spoon, worried that it might burn me, but it was just warm enough without being too hot. And it tasted delicious.

'Very nice,' I said.

'Excellent,' he replied. 'Then I suggest you take a seat while I finish the meal. Alice, I hope you're not intending straining the potatoes yourself. That's no job for a woman. Sit down, pour yourself a glass of wine and let me wait on you, for heaven's sake.'

I went over to the table where Luke was sitting and he nodded at me.

'All right,' he said.

'All right,' I replied. 'I didn't ask to come, you know,' I told him under my breath. 'She came over and got me.'

'I don't care,' he said. 'You think it matters to me who she invites for dinner? It's still my dad's house, no matter what.'

'Danny?' asked Mrs Kennedy and I turned to look at her. I had the feeling she'd said my name a couple of times already and I hadn't heard her. 'What would you like to drink?'

'I don't mind,' I said. 'A glass of water.'

'I think we can do better than that, don't you? A Coke perhaps? Or an orange juice?' she asked.

'Coke,' I said quickly.

'Coke it is. Luke, what do you want?'

'Don't care,' grunted Luke.

'Fine,' said Mrs Kennedy, putting a glass of Coke on the table before me. 'Well when you do care, you know where the fridge is and you can help yourself.'

'Coke rots the teeth,' said Mr Benson and I turned to look at him, worried that I'd disappointed him somehow, but he didn't look angry. 'But I can't start the day without a glass. It's an addiction. For some people, it's coffee.' He glared at Mrs Kennedy when he said that but she just laughed. 'For others, it's cigarettes.' He glared at her again, fiercely, and she laughed again and shook her head. I didn't know whether he was joking or not, but I supposed he must have been, because she seemed to find it funny. 'But for me, it's Coke. What about you, Luke? What are your addictions?'

'Are we actually eating tonight?' asked Luke, glaring at him. 'Or just talking about it?'

'A hungry man,' said Mr Benson, putting the steaks on the plates with some potatoes and vegetables. Then he poured the mushroom sauce over the meat and put them down in front of us. He sat opposite me while Luke and his mam faced each other at both ends.

'To the chef,' said Mr Benson, raising his glass. 'Oh hold on,' he added, as if he'd forgotten something. 'That's me. How rude.'

Mrs Kennedy laughed and I giggled, but Luke looked like he was getting ready to kill someone, so I tried to wipe the smile off my face in case it turned out to be me.

'And what did you do today, Danny?' asked Mrs Kennedy. 'Anything good?'

'I went cycling,' I told her.

'I can't cycle any more,' said Mr Benson. 'I'm too big for the bikes. I'd crush them.'

'I used to love cycling when I was a girl,' said Mrs Kennedy. 'That's where I met David, actually,' she added. 'On a cycling holiday in

France.'

'David's my father,' said Luke, even though I knew. 'This is his house.'

'Actually, this is *my* house,' said Mrs Kennedy, staring at her son. 'Mine and yours.'

Mr Benson and I exchanged a glance but said nothing. I tried to imagine what it would be like if Dad didn't live with us, didn't even see us like Luke's dad almost never saw him, but I couldn't do it. I couldn't imagine our house without him. Or Mam.

I looked down at my food and, even though I was starving, I found that I didn't have much of an appetite.

'What's wrong, Danny?' asked Mrs Kennedy. 'Aren't you hungry?'

I looked down at my plate and shook my head. I started counting from one to ten in my mind as quickly as I could, because I could feel tears behind my eyes and knew that I might start crying at any moment.

'You'll get ill if you don't eat,' she said.

'Ah, look at him,' shouted Luke triumphantly. 'He's crying!'

'I'm not!' I shouted as a tear hit the plate. I spun around to glare at him and could feel my chin trembling even as the tears came. I put my hand up to wipe them away.

'Luke, be quiet,' snapped Mrs Kennedy.

'I'm sorry,' I said.

'You have nothing to be sorry for,' said Mrs Kennedy, standing up. 'Nothing at all. Come in to the living room with me for a minute. We're going to take a few quiet moments for ourselves. And Luke, I don't want to hear a peep out of you while we're gone. Is that understood?'

Luke nodded and looked a little sheepish as his mam took my hand and led me out of the kitchen. I glanced back as she shut the door

behind us and saw him and Mr
Benson staring at each other.

'More mushroom sauce, Luke?'
asked Mr Benson.

CHAPTER FOUR

We were watching television later that night when the phone rang and Mrs Kennedy went out to answer it. She talked in the hallway for a few minutes before poking her head back around the door.

'Danny,' she said. 'It's your dad. He wants to talk to you.'

'Hello,' I said, speaking nervously into the receiver.

'Hi,' said Dad. 'Sorry we weren't there when you got home.'

'It's all right,' I said, even though it wasn't.

'You've had your dinner?'

'Yes.'

'Good. Then I need you to do something for me.'

'What?'

'You don't mind staying in Mrs Kennedy's house tonight, do you?'

My heart sank. I wanted to be at

home. I wanted us all to be at home together.

'Why?' I asked. 'Where are you?'

He paused. 'Didn't I say?'

'No.'

'We're at the hospital, Danny,' he said quietly. 'Your mam's a little off-colour, I told you that.'

I opened my mouth to say something else but before I could, the phone was taken out of my hands by Mrs Kennedy, who had appeared beside me without making a sound.

'Russell?' she said and she sounded very determined now. 'It's Alice again. Listen, there's nothing to worry about. We're all watching television and Danny's going to be absolutely fine here. You and Rachel just take care of yourselves, all right?' There was a pause and I could hear a voice on the other end of the phone but I couldn't make out the words. Mrs Kennedy shook her head before speaking again. 'I can always take the day off,' she said.

Another pause. 'Well I can if you need me to,' she said. Another pause. 'All right, then we'll see you in the morning.' She looked in my direction and seemed to make a decision because she turned away from me. 'Danny says goodnight,' she said, even though I'd said nothing of the sort. 'We'll see you tomorrow. Goodnight, Russell.'

She put the phone down and turned back to me.

'Listen,' she said, reading my mind. 'Think of it as an adventure.'

'But where will I sleep?' I asked her.

'In Luke's room,' she said. 'He has bunk beds.'

That sounded better. I nodded. 'Which one does he sleep in?' I asked.

'Which one do you want to sleep in?' she asked me.

I thought about it. 'The top one,' I said.

'Then he sleeps in the bottom

one,' she said, winking at me. 'Come on, let's go into the sitting room. My programme's coming on.'

*   *   *

Later that night, Mrs Kennedy took bed sheets, pillows and a duvet out of a cupboard and made up the top bunk. After that, she took a pair of Luke's pyjamas out of a drawer and gave them to me and the three of us stared awkwardly at each other for a minute before Mrs Kennedy took the hint.

'I'll be back up in a few minutes to make sure you're all settled in,' she said. 'I've left a fresh toothbrush in the bathroom, Danny. You'll see it sitting by the sink still in its wrapper, so you don't have to worry.'

I went in to the bathroom and cleaned my teeth slowly. When I came out, I saw a half-open door to my left and peeped inside. It was Mrs Kennedy's bedroom. The lights were off, the curtains were open and the light from the moon was shining through, giving it a sort of brightness that was half dark and half shadows. I knew I shouldn't go inside but I couldn't help it, so I walked in. Mrs Kennedy's bed was very big, bigger even than Mam and Dad's. To the right there was a dressing table with so many bottles and lotions on it that I wondered how she knew which was which. I walked towards the window and stared through it, and I could see into my own bedroom on the other side of the fence because my curtains were open. I stared at the place where I'd stood and watched Mrs Kennedy. I remembered where I'd been standing the night I saw her in her bra. I could see the posters on my bedroom walls and the dirty T-shirt I'd left hanging over the side of my chair.

If Mam was home, I thought, that would have been in the laundry by now.

'You finished in there?' asked Luke when I came back in to the bedroom, and I nodded. He was in his pyjamas now and marched past me towards the bathroom, closing the door behind him, and I pulled my clothes off as quickly as I could and got into the set that Mrs Kennedy had left for me. When he came back in I was folding my trousers and shirt neatly and putting them on the back of the chair. I climbed up the ladder in to the top bunk and got under the duvet.

'Benjamin's an idiot, isn't he?' said Luke.

'Mr Benson?' I asked. 'He's all right. He looks like a polar bear.'

'He shouldn't be here,' said Luke. 'What right does he have to cook dinner for us anyway? It's not his house. It's my dad's house. When I go to stay with him this summer, I'm going to tell him.'

I turned over on to my back and looked up at the ceiling and saw that it was covered with hundreds of tiny stars that had been stuck there and glowed in the dark. It was how I imagined sleeping out on the top of a mountain would be. I stretched my arm out to touch them, but my fingers couldn't quite reach.

'What's happening at your house?' asked Luke after a few moments.

'Nothing,' I said.

'Of course there is. Tell me.'

'*Nothing*,' I insisted, wishing he wouldn't ask me about it.

He snorted. 'That's not what I heard,' he said.

'What did you hear?'

'I heard your mam got drunk and knocked someone down and killed him.'

I sat up in bed. 'That's not true,' I said.

'My mam said it.'

'She did?' I asked, shocked.

'Well, no,' admitted Luke. 'She didn't say she killed him. But she said that he was probably going to die. That he's in a coma and there isn't much hope. I heard her saying it before you got here.'

I lay down again and stared at the stars, feeling sick inside. There was a tap on the door and it opened, only a little at first and then all the way, and a beam of light came through, followed by Mrs Kennedy.

'Are you boys all right?' she asked. 'You have everything you need, Danny?'

'Is Danny staying here tomorrow night?' asked Luke.

'I don't know,' said Mrs Kennedy. 'We'll see.'

'Am I?' I asked, startled, wondering how long this was going to go on for.

'Don't worry about it,' she said. 'Get some sleep. We'll know more tomorrow. Now you're not to stay up talking all night, do you hear me? It's late.'

She leaned over the bottom bunk and I could hear her kissing Luke goodnight.

'Goodnight Danny,' she said then, smiling across at me. 'You know where I am if you need me.'

'It's the second door on the right,' said Luke.

'Oh, he knows,' said Mrs Kennedy. I could see her smiling in the moonlight as she left, and even though it was dark I could feel my face grow bright red.

Luke and I didn't say anything for a long time, and after a while I thought I heard the sound of his breathing change as he rolled over, and I thought that maybe he was asleep.

'She wasn't drunk,' I whispered.

CHAPTER FIVE

'Of course she wasn't drunk,' said Dad when I told him the story the next day. 'For heaven's sake, Danny, when have you ever seen your mam drunk in your whole life? Do you even know what drunk is?'

'It's what Pete's friends always are when they stay over,' I said.

'Hmm,' said Dad, grunting as he took his glasses off to read the instructions on a packet of spaghetti. 'Well that's true enough. But you should know your mam better than that. It was an accident. That's all. The police know it. The parents of the little boy know it. And even your mam knows it.'

'Then why is she so upset?' I asked.

'Because although it wasn't her fault, she still feels responsible. You can understand that, can't you?

Look, she was driving home from the shops, coming down Parker Grove. A witness saw the whole thing. She said that your mam wasn't even driving fast but this little boy, Andy, came charging out from a house. He ran out on to the road without looking left or right. There was no way she could have stopped in time. We're not sure what the little boy was even doing there. It wasn't even his house. He lives a few doors down on the other side of the street.'

'Maybe he was lost,' I suggested.

'Well, we'll find out in due course, I'm sure.'

'Is he going to die?' I asked and Dad shook his head.

'Why don't you go outside,' he said. 'Dinner's not for another hour yet.'

I sighed and went in to the garden. My bike was standing where I'd left it, propped up against the fence between our house and Luke Kennedy's. I jumped on the saddle and that's when I saw her for the first time. She'd been watching me from across the road, standing beside a tree. She had pale red hair, down to her shoulders, and was wearing blue jeans with a large white pattern of a daisy printed across one of the knees. She was about the same age as me but I didn't know her so she couldn't have been in my school.

I didn't slow down but I stared at her, wondering why she was watching me, as I cycled down the road, turned the corner and vanished out of sight.

*   *   *

I got a puncture when I was out and didn't have anything to fix it with, so I ended up having to wheel my bike all the way home again. I always took the short cut through the estate when I was coming home, but that day I took a different route. I went down Parker Grove, the road that Mam had been driving on when the little boy had run out in front of her.

It was a street like ours with a lot of trees outside the houses. I didn't know which was Andy's house, but as I was making my way along, wheeling my bike beside me, a car pulled into a driveway and a woman came running across the road.

'Michael, Samantha,' she called towards the couple who were getting out of the car. 'How's Andy doing? Is there any news?'

'He's . . . well, he's no worse,' said the woman, Samantha, quietly. 'The doctors say that's a good sign. They always say the first forty-eight hours are critical, don't they?'

'Well, no worse is better than nothing,' said the woman. 'He's bound to wake up soon.'

'If only he would respond to something we do,' said Samantha then, shaking her head in frustration. 'We talk to him all the time. We play the songs he likes on the stereo. This morning we set up a video of some cartoon that he watches and played it over and over but there's nothing. It's as if . . .'

Her voice trailed off and she started to cry. I turned the wheel of my bike a few more times and saw a piece of glass wedged in the tyre. I hadn't really been looking for the puncture but I'd found it anyway. I put my fingers carefully on either side of it and pulled the shard of glass out and the tyre began to hiss, which made me think I should have left it in until I got home.

'And how's Sarah coping with it?' asked the woman and I heard Andy's mam sniffling like she had a bad cold. It was the kind of sound that, whenever I made it, Mam told me to get a handkerchief and not to be so disgusting.

'I don't know,' she said. 'She's gone very quiet. She won't speak to either of us about it. I've never known her to be so detached from something before.'

She stopped talking then, and I looked up and saw the two women standing at the bottom of the driveway, staring at me.

'Are you all right?' asked Andy's mam.

'Fine,' I said.

'What are you doing down there?'

I coughed and tried to make myself look as innocent as possible. 'It's my bike,' I said, standing up. 'It had a puncture. I was trying to see if I could find it.' They went on staring at me and I put my hands on the handlebars and started to wheel it forward. 'I'll have to bring it home to fix it.'

Neither of them spoke, but they watched me as I walked off; it took me about two minutes to get to the end of the road and I could feel their eyes on my back all the way. Normally I would have cycled off as quickly as possible, but that wasn't possible with the puncture.

Eventually I turned the corner, but it still took me about twenty minutes to get back to our street. She was waiting there. The girl with the red hair. She was sitting at the top of the road with her back to a tree and I knew she was waiting for me. I couldn't think why. I didn't remember ever seeing her before today. Somehow I just knew that she wanted to talk to me.

I slowed down as I got closer and she looked round and watched me, and then stood up, dusting down the back of her jeans with her hands as she did so. I turned my head away, wondering whether she would still be watching when I turned back, and she was. Normally I didn't like to talk to girls because they always looked at me like I'd just crawled out from under a rock. But I knew I had to stop and talk to this particular girl. I knew there was no way out of it.

'Hi,' I said when I was only a few

feet away from her, stopping now and holding the bike between us.

'Are you Danny?' she asked.

'Yes.'

'I knew it was you,' she said then. 'I saw you earlier.'

'You were waiting outside the house,' I said. 'You were watching me.'

She opened her mouth, looking like she was going to disagree with me, but then she shrugged her shoulders as if she couldn't be bothered. 'Yes,' she said. 'Yes, I was.'

And then it hit me and I knew exactly who she was.

'You're Sarah, aren't you?' I asked her. 'Andy's sister?'

She nodded and I couldn't help but think that I'd spent some of that afternoon spying on her family, while she'd spent nearly all the day spying on mine. And only now, when the day was nearly over, were we finally getting to talk to each other. It was like we were secret agents and we'd got bored of it all and just decided to come clean.

CHAPTER SIX

It was the Saturday after Sarah had first shown up outside our house and we'd arranged to meet in the park. I was sitting on a bench near the fountain, reading *David Copperfield*. I wanted her to see that I read books like this. After a few minutes, I saw her coming through the gates opposite me. I smiled and waved. It surprised me how happy I was to see her.

'I wasn't sure if you'd be here,' she said when she sat down. 'I thought you might change your mind about coming.'

'No,' I said, shaking my head. 'I promised, didn't I?'

'I thought I was going to be late. Mam was going to the hospital to see Andy and she wanted me to come too and, when I said I couldn't, she got mad with me.'

'Do you go often?' I asked her.

'Every day. Sometimes twice a day. Do you have any brothers or sisters?'

'I have an older brother,' I told her. 'Pete. He's eighteen and in university in Edinburgh. He was supposed to come home for the summer holidays. He promised me he would, but then he changed his mind and went travelling around Europe instead.'

Sarah nodded. 'Andy's my only brother too,' she said.

I wanted to ask her how he was but didn't know how to phrase it. I knew it wasn't my fault that he was in hospital, but somehow I felt responsible for it.

'Is he going to get better?' I asked her.

'We don't know,' she said. 'We just have to hope that he wakes up soon.'

'He will,' I said.

'How do you know?'

'I just do,' I told her. She didn't seem too happy with me saying that and looked a little angry, so I bit my lip and decided I'd better think about things more carefully in future before I said them. She didn't seem like the kind of girl who just made idle conversation.

'How did you know who I was?' she asked me after a few more minutes had passed. 'When I came to your house, I mean. You guessed immediately.'

'I don't know,' I said. 'It just seemed to make sense. Why did you come?'

'I was interested, that's all. It was your mam I was looking for really. I wanted to see what she looked like. And then I saw you. Everything's been so terrible these last few days.' She leaned forward and put her face in her hands for a moment and I was worried that she was going to start crying. I didn't know what I'd do if she did. There was no way I was going to put my arm around her. Not here, where anyone could see us. But when she lifted her face again, she just stared at me and shook her head.

'It's not your mam's fault anyway,' she said. 'That's what's so terrible about all of this. It's my fault. But I can't tell anyone. And I don't know what to do to make it better.'

I frowned, uncertain what she could mean by this. I opened my mouth to ask her but, just as I did, I saw three people walking along the path towards us. My stomach sank a little but it was too late to get away from them. It was Luke Kennedy, with his mother and Benjamin Benson.

'Danny,' said Mrs Kennedy when she reached us, looking at Sarah for a moment as if she was surprised to see me sitting there with a girl—as if this was the last thing in the world she would ever have expected. Even though I'd grown an inch and a half over the last three months, not that anyone had noticed except me.

'Hello,' I said, trying not to look at Luke, who was staring at Sarah. 'I just came out for a walk.'

'You're not going to get much walking done sitting down,' said Mr Benson cheerfully. 'Lots of exercise, that's what a boy your age needs. That and a good solid breakfast every morning. And an ice-cold bath once a year whether you need one or not.'

I frowned. I didn't know why he had to be so cheerful all the time, unless it was to impress Mrs Kennedy.

'Aren't you going to introduce us to your friend?' asked Mrs Kennedy and I stared at her, not knowing what to say. I didn't want to tell her the truth in case she told Mam or Dad and I got into trouble. Although I wasn't sure exactly what I was doing wrong, it felt like I was doing something that they wouldn't be happy about.

'We're not friends,' said Sarah

quickly. 'I was just sitting here, that's all.'

'Oh, I'm sorry,' said Mrs Kennedy. 'You looked so cosy there, the two of you. I didn't like to interrupt at first.'

'Chatting her up, I dare say,' said Mr Benson. 'Oh, don't look so embarrassed, Danny. We all have to start somewhere.'

'You told me you were busy,' said Luke, pointing a finger at me. 'You said that was why you couldn't come out today.'

'I have to go,' said Sarah suddenly, standing up. I looked at her, not wanting her to leave. I wanted Luke and Mrs Kennedy and Mr Benson to keep walking, and to stop trying to say funny or embarrassing things. I wanted to talk to Sarah on her own and have her tell me why the accident hadn't been Mam's fault at all and why she thought it was hers.

'Wait,' I said, but Luke interrupted me.

'Let's go and get the bikes,' he

said. 'We'll go out somewhere. Just the two of us,' he added.

'Goodbye,' said Sarah, starting to move off.

'Wait,' I repeated, but she shook her head.

'You don't have to leave on our account,' said Mrs Kennedy, who looked sorry now that she had stopped to talk to us in the first place.

'Bye,' shouted Luke to Sarah. 'See you around sometime. Or not.'

She stopped and stared at him for a moment before walking on. He frowned, unsure how to handle a look like that.

'Sorry about that, old man,' said Mr Benson. 'Looks like we chased her away.'

*   *   *

I stayed out later than normal that night and when I came home I found Dad sitting in the living room, watching television. He glanced at his watch when I came in and looked a little surprised by how late it was.

'Danny,' he said. 'It's nearly ten o'clock.'

'I know,' I replied.

'What were you doing out until this time?'

I shrugged my shoulders and sat down. 'Sorry,' I said. 'I lost track of time.'

'So did I, actually,' he said quietly. 'I didn't even realize it or I would have started to worry about you.'

'Where's Mam?'

'You just missed her,' he said. 'She's having an early night.'

'Has she been in bed all day?' I asked angrily. 'She was in bed when I left this afternoon!'

'Danny, she got up shortly after you left. We had dinner together. We watched some television and, if you had come home on time like you were supposed to, then you would have seen her and you could have

56

talked to her. And by the way, while we're on the subject, I'd appreciate it if you did a little more of that anyway.'

I nodded and thought about going to bed, but before I could he laughed suddenly and turned back to me.

'Oh, by the way,' he said. 'I talked to your gran today. She and Granddad are coming to visit next week. For your birthday. I thought we'd have a small party.'

'A party?' I asked, surprised. 'Are you sure?'

'Oh, just family, that's all,' he said quickly. 'Your mother and I, your grandparents. We can ask the Kennedys too, if you like.'

'I don't know if I want a party,' I said.

'A party's the wrong word,' he said, shaking his head. 'It's a dinner, nothing more than that. A family dinner. Next Thursday. We have to eat, after all. Don't look so worried! It'll be fun.'

I shrugged. I wasn't really thinking about it anyway. I was wondering when—and if—I'd ever get to see Sarah again, and whether I'd ever find out why she thought that everything had been her fault and not Mam's. Maybe if I found out, I decided, I could tell Mam and then she wouldn't be so upset any more and everything could get back to normal.

Somehow, I knew I had to find out Sarah's secret.

CHAPTER SEVEN

There were eight seats set around the dinner table and I was at the head since it was my birthday. Dad was sitting at the other end so he could go in and out of the kitchen whenever he realized he'd forgotten something. Gran and Granddad sat along one side with an empty seat between them; that was where Mam was supposed to be. And facing them were Luke Kennedy, his mam and Benjamin Benson, who was keeping the conversation alive.

'My father spent most of the war in jail,' he told us. 'He was a conscientious objector, you see. He couldn't stand all that fighting. He was a pacifist all his life.'

'Really,' said Granddad, raising an eyebrow. Something told me he didn't think too much of people who'd done that, but we'd read about them in school and I wasn't so sure.

'Spent half his life on peace marches,' Mr Benson continued. 'Got himself thrown in the slammer again during the seventies, when that old warmonger Nixon came to visit. That's what got me interested in the law, you see. The way they treated a simple man who didn't want to hurt anybody.'

'You're quite right,' said Granddad cheerfully. 'It probably would have been a damn sight better if we'd all ended up speaking German and goose-stepping around Trafalgar Square.'

It was a quarter past seven already and Mam was fifteen minutes late and no one was saying anything about it.

'Did you get any nice presents, Danny?' asked Mrs Kennedy.

'I didn't get anything,' I said, shaking my head as if I couldn't quite believe it myself.

'You didn't get *anything*?' asked

Luke in amazement. 'On your birthday?'

'Now that's not true, Danny,' said Dad quickly. 'Your gran brought you a lovely jumper, didn't she?'

'Oh yes,' I said, remembering the green knitted jumper that I'd put in my wardrobe earlier and that I would never, on pain of death, wear. 'That's right, I forgot. And Granddad gave me some money.'

'Money?' asked Gran, staring at Granddad and pursing her lips. 'What did I tell you?'

'Oh it was just a few pounds for the lad,' said Granddad dismissively. 'Dry up, woman.'

'I have something outside for you, Danny,' said Mrs Kennedy. 'It's not much, just a book. I'll give it to you after dinner.'

'And I forgot to give you this,' said Dad, reaching across to the sideboard and handing me an envelope. 'It came second post.'

I smiled when I saw the familiar

handwriting. There was a 'Happy Retirement' card inside rather than a birthday card, which was the kind of thing that Pete always did because he thought it was funny. He never got the right card for the right occasion. There was a ten-pound note in it too. I read the card quickly and felt relieved, as I thought he'd forgotten about me until then. I'd wondered whether he'd show up for the party, but he'd called a couple of nights before from Amsterdam and he wasn't making any sense at all on the phone. Dad took it off me and told him not to bother again until he got his head clear.

'So why did you say you didn't get anything?' asked Luke.

'He meant that he didn't get anything from his mam and me,' explained Dad. 'We'll take him out over the weekend and buy him something special then.'

'But that's not the same thing,' said Luke. 'You have to get it on your birthday or it doesn't count.'

'Be quiet, Luke, and eat your dinner,' said Mrs Kennedy.

'But we haven't been given any dinner yet,' he said in surprise, and I had to bite my lip to stop myself from laughing.

'He's quite right,' said Dad, looking at his watch. 'She's twenty-five minutes late now.'

'She'll be here, Russell,' said Gran.

'I'm glad you feel so confident.'

'One of us should have gone out with her,' said Gran. 'Made sure she was all right.'

'Maybe I should go take a look for her,' suggested Mrs Kennedy. 'Perhaps she went for a walk.'

'You don't want to go walking around here too late at night,' said Benjamin Benson, scratching his beard. 'You're likely to get yourself mugged or killed or worse.'

'Your father has a funny way of looking at things,' Granddad told Luke.

'He's not my father,' said Luke.

'I could just take a quick walk around the neighbourhood and see if I can—'

'No!' said Dad, slapping a hand down on the table and making everyone jump. No one said anything for a moment. We just stared at him. 'She's half an hour late now and we're all hungry and besides, it's Danny's birthday. It's time to eat. Belinda,' he said, looking across at Gran. 'Perhaps you'd help me serve up the meal.'

And with that he went in to the kitchen and I knew that the eighth seat at my birthday dinner would be remaining empty for the night.

*　　　*　　　*

By a quarter to nine we were eating the birthday cake when the door opened and quietly, like a ghost, Mam entered the room.

'What's going on?' she asked. 'Oh

64

yes, I forgot. You were cooking tonight, weren't you?'

'For seven o'clock,' Dad said. 'You said you'd be home by then.'

'I got delayed,' she said. 'I'm sorry, I—'

'It's not good enough,' he said, his voice holding firm. 'It's not good enough at all. It's Danny's birthday and you said that you'd—'

'Russell, I said I'm sorry,' she snapped. 'I got delayed.'

'You were never coming.'

'Oh just shut up, Russell, for God's sake,' she snapped and we all jumped, except for Dad who remained perfectly still before standing up and walking over to her.

'Don't. Shout. At. Me,' he said clearly, pausing between his words.

'Rachel, dear, why don't you sit down and I'll heat you up some—'

'She can't have any,' said Dad, turning to look at Gran, who immediately fell quiet and nodded, knowing who was in charge here. 'If she can't make it home in time for dinner, then she doesn't get any.'

I heard Mam gasp but didn't want to look at her. She gasped again, almost laughing. 'If I don't get here in time, I can't *have* any?' she asked, amazed. 'What am I, eight years old? Yes, Mother, if you could heat some up for me that would be lovely.'

'Stay where you are, Belinda,' said Dad, who stepped up close to my mother now, saying nothing, just staring at her as if he hardly knew her any more. We all watched, holding our breaths. This time when she spoke, her voice cracked a little, as if she knew that there was a long-awaited battle coming up but she really wanted to put it off. Just for another day or so. Just until she felt a little stronger.

'I'm sorry,' she said quietly, her eyes filling with tears.

'I've had enough of this, Rachel,' said Dad. 'We all have.'

'*You've* had enough?' she shouted,

finding her voice again suddenly. This was who she was now, I realized. From one moment to the next, I never knew what to expect. '*You've* had enough? *You* don't have all of this weighing down on your conscience, Russell. *You* didn't nearly kill a child. *You* don't have to live with that, do you?'

'And neither do you,' he said, remaining firm. 'It was an accident. The boy is still alive. And Danny is alive too, in case you hadn't noticed. And Pete is alive. What about the kids, Rachel? Can't you think about them for once?'

I turned in my chair to look at her, feeling the tears beneath my lids now too. She looked at me for a moment and shook her head.

'There's only one who matters,' she said, and I knew she didn't mean me. I normally would have thought she meant Pete because he was her favourite, but tonight I knew the only kid who mattered was Andy.

*   *   *

It was much later that night, past eleven o'clock. I was wheeling the bins outside for the morning collection when I heard a voice whispering my name.

'Danny!' the voice said. 'Danny! Over here!'

I glanced around quickly, trying to make out where it was coming from, and just as I did so, she stepped out from behind a tree.

'Sarah,' I said, walking towards her. 'You came back.'

'I'm sorry,' she told me. 'I wasn't sure if I should.'

'I'm glad you did.'

'I can't stay very long,' she said. 'If they find out I'm not at home there'll be trouble.'

I nodded. I wanted to tell her that it was my birthday, but I couldn't find a way to say it. I wondered what she'd do if she knew. Whether she'd kiss me.

'There was something I wanted to ask you,' she said.

'What?'

'What are you doing on Monday?'

'Nothing,' I said.

'I'm going to the hospital on my own that afternoon,' she told me. 'Mam and Dad won't be there till night-time. Will you come with me?'

I hesitated, unsure whether I really wanted to see what Mam had done to her brother or not. I stared down at the ground, knowing this might be a bad idea.

'Please, Danny,' she said. 'I'd like you to see him.'

'Why did you say it was all your fault?' I asked her.

'What?'

'That day in the park. You said it was your fault, not Mam's. What did you mean by that?'

Now it was her turn to hesitate, and she looked away for a moment before turning back to me and nodding. 'Because—' she began, but before she could say anything else the side door opened and I heard Dad stepping outside.

'Danny?' he called. 'Danny, are you out here? What's keeping you?'

'Four o'clock on Monday,' whispered Sarah, grabbing my arm. 'I'll see you outside the hospital then. I'll explain everything, I promise.'

And with that she darted off down the street.

'Danny,' said Dad, coming up to me. 'What are you doing standing out here on your own? Come back inside.'

I nodded. 'I was just coming,' I said.

CHAPTER EIGHT

I arrived at the hospital ahead of time and Sarah was already waiting for me. 'He's in a private room,' she said as we stepped into the lift and went up to the sixth floor. 'So you don't have to worry about anyone catching you. I'm glad you came,' she added. 'I hate visiting on my own.'

We went in to his room and I stared at the little boy in the bed. He looked like he was fast asleep. If it hadn't been for all the hospital equipment that he was connected to, I would have sworn that I could have just shaken him by the shoulders and woken him up. There was a drip running from a bag on a hook into his arm. A machine on his right-hand side had a screen on it. The numbers and lines kept changing and it gave a bip-bip-bip sound every so often.

'This is Andy,' said Sarah. 'What's

the matter?' she asked, turning to look at me.

'Shouldn't we keep the noise down?' I said. 'We don't want to disturb him.'

She laughed and I realized how stupid this had sounded. 'Danny, if he hears us and wakes up, well that's a good thing, remember?'

'Of course,' I said. 'Sorry.'

'Don't you want to say hello to him?' she asked me then.

'To Andy?'

'Yes.'

I looked down at him and swallowed nervously. He had a small, round face and his hair was the same shade of red as Sarah's. He had a few freckles around his nose too. His mouth was open and he was wearing Rupert Bear pyjamas, the same ones I used to have when I was small.

'Hi Andy,' I said, feeling awkward and embarrassed.

'Andy,' said Sarah. 'This is my friend Danny. He's come to visit you.'

'Do you think he can hear us?' I asked her, and she shrugged her shoulders.

'The doctors say he can. And even if he can't, it doesn't do any harm to talk to him, does it? It's better than sitting here saying nothing.'

'I suppose so,' I said. 'He doesn't look like he's in any pain, does he?'

'No,' she said, shaking her head and looking very sad. 'I hope he isn't anyway.'

'My brother Pete was in hospital once,' I told her, 'when he had his appendix out. He missed the last few weeks of school because of it. He went around for days saying he had a pain in his stomach and no one believed him. Then one night it exploded inside him and he could have died, only he didn't, but he did get to ride in an ambulance. I don't know what Mam would have done if he hadn't got better, because he's her favourite.'

I turned around when I realized that Sarah wasn't standing beside me any more. She was sitting in an armchair in the corner of the room, holding her face in her hands.

'Sarah,' I said quietly, walking towards her. 'Are you all right?'

'It was only supposed to be a game,' she said, looking up at me now. Her face was pale but her eyes were dry. 'It wasn't supposed to end like this.'

'What was?' I asked her. 'What was a game?'

'The afternoon that he got hit,' she said. 'We were always playing games like that, giving each other dares to do. He always did whatever I told him.'

I wanted to sit down but the only place to sit was on the side of Andy's bed and I didn't think that would be right.

'That afternoon,' she went on. 'I told him about "knock down ginger". You've played that, right?'

'Of course,' I said. 'Ringing doorbells and running away. I used to do it all the time.'

'The house across the road from us,' she continued. 'Number 42. They have a big dog and when you walk past you can hear it inside because it barks really loudly. I dared Andy to go across and creep up the driveway without the dog hearing him, then ring the doorbell and run away. I said I'd watch him from my bedroom window upstairs. And he said he'd do it. He walked up the driveway and when he got to the door he turned around and looked up and gave me a big smile and the thumbs-up to say the dog wasn't barking. Then he turned back and put his finger on the doorbell. The second he rang it, I knew the dog had gone crazy inside because he nearly jumped out of his skin. He got such a fright, in fact, that he leapt away from the door and ran straight out on to the road without thinking and when he did . . .

when he ran out there . . . that's when . . .'

She buried her face in her hands again and this time I could hear her sobbing.

'Sarah,' I said, coming towards her, unsure what to do to console her.

'You see, Danny?' she said, looking up. 'The whole thing's my fault. If I hadn't been playing that stupid game with him, if I hadn't dared him to play knock down ginger on the door of number 42—'

'Then Mam would never have hit him,' I said, finishing her sentence for her. I started to feel angry, thinking about it. 'She thinks it was all her fault. But it wasn't, was it?'

I wanted to say more, to tell her how things were at home because of her stupid game, but I could hear voices suddenly, just outside the room, and Sarah and I looked towards the door at the same moment and then back at each other in fright.

'Mam and Dad,' she said, her face growing even whiter now. 'You've got to hide. They'll go mad if they find you here. Under the bed!'

'What?'

'Get under the bed,' she insisted. 'The sheets go all the way to the floor. They'll never see you there.'

I turned and looked at the bed and at Andy lying in it. The last place I wanted to be was underneath there.

'I can't,' I said, shaking my head. 'I can't do it.'

'Danny, you have to,' she insisted, and the door opened slightly and we could hear a woman's voice talking to a doctor outside. 'Quick!' she said, pushing me towards it, and before I knew what was happening I was sliding across the floor and crawling under the bed. The moment I did, I heard the door open fully and the sound of four feet coming in to the room.

'Sarah, there you are,' said a woman's voice. I felt her get very close to where I was and guessed that she was leaning down to kiss Andy—because I could smell her perfume—and then she said 'Hello, my darling' under her breath.

'Have you been crying?' asked her father.

'A little bit,' said Sarah.

'I hate seeing you so upset,' said her mam, sighing loudly. 'When I think about what that woman has done to this family . . .'

My lip curled a little in anger. I hoped she wasn't going to start saying mean things about Mam or I wouldn't know what to do.

'We spoke to Dr Harris,' said her father. 'He said that Andy is still stable at the moment, which is a good sign. At least he isn't getting any worse.'

'We might as well tell her, Michael.'

'Tell me what?' asked Sarah.

There was a brief pause and then her father spoke again. 'We were at the police station this afternoon,' he said. 'They've confirmed that they won't be pressing any charges against Rachel Delaney.'

'Can you believe it?' said her mam furiously. 'That maniac goes racing down our road, practically kills my little boy, and they're not even going to charge her for it. What kind of justice system do we have anyway when someone can—'

'Samantha, they explained it to us. It wasn't entirely her fault.'

'Oh what, so you're saying it was Andy's fault?' she asked. 'You're blaming him for what happened?'

'Of course I'm not blaming him. I'm just saying that if—'

'It's absolutely ridiculous,' she shouted. 'That woman, that bloody woman with no sense of right or wrong does this and she gets away with it scot-free. Well I'm not having it. If I have to go around there myself and—'

I couldn't listen to any more. I

scrambled out from under the bed, almost hitting my head on the metal frame as I did so. Sarah's father shouted in surprise and her mam jumped back as if she'd just seen a mouse.

'It wasn't her!' I yelled at them, feeling my face grow red now with anger. 'It was Sarah. Why don't you ask her what really happened and then you'll—'

I stopped myself from saying anything else. We all looked at each other, not knowing what to say. There was only one thing I could do.

I ran.

CHAPTER NINE

'Danny,' said Dad later that afternoon, coming in to my bedroom without even knocking. 'Tell me you didn't do it.'

'Didn't do what?' I asked, looking at him as if I really didn't know.

'You know very well what,' he said. 'And I can tell by the expression on your face that you did it, too. What on earth were you thinking of?'

'I don't know what you're talking about, I—'

'Oh don't play the innocent,' he snapped. 'I've just had the police at the front door and it was all I could do to persuade them to let *me* and not *them* talk to you about this. Apparently Mr and Mrs Maclean reported you for trespassing in their son's hospital room. Tell me it's not true, for pity's sake. Tell me they've got it wrong.'

I hung my head in shame. For a couple of moments I actually considered telling him that yes, they had got it completely wrong, that I hadn't gone anywhere near the hospital. Why would I, after all? And I could probably get Luke Kennedy to provide me with an alibi if I really needed one. But there was no way out of it. I had to come clean.

'It's not how it looks,' I began, but he cut me off and threw his arms in the air in frustration.

'I don't believe it,' he shouted. 'Don't you think we've had enough of policemen coming to this house with bad news for one lifetime? What on earth were you thinking of? What were you even doing there?'

'I wanted to see him,' I said. 'Sarah said that she'd like me to and—'

'Sarah?' he asked, staring at me in surprise. 'Who on earth is Sarah? I've never heard you mention her before.'

'Sarah Maclean,' I told him.

'Andy's sister.'

'Andy's . . .' He thought about this for a moment and sat down on the bed where he started to shake his head, laughing a little. 'You're friends with that little boy's sister? And you never told me this before?'

'I'm not friends with her,' I explained. 'At least, I didn't know her before this all started. She came here. A couple of weeks ago.'

'She came to our house?'

'She waited outside on the street. I saw her watching me. We talked for a bit and then we met up in the park and we talked again there. And then she came by after my birthday party.' I mentioned that, hoping it would win me some sympathy, considering how that evening had turned out. 'She's nice,' I added, even though I wasn't sure why I needed to tell him that.

'I don't care how nice she is,' said Dad. 'She has no more business coming here than you have visiting her brother in the hospital. How do you think your mother would feel if she ran into her and found out who she was?'

'That's not a very good choice of words,' I said.

'*Don't* get smart with me,' said Dad, standing up and pointing a finger at me. He looked really angry now and I wished I hadn't said that. 'How do you think that poor boy's parents felt when you jumped out from underneath his bed?'

'Oh, I'm sick of him!' I shouted. 'Isn't everyone sick of him? I wish he'd just die, if he's going to die, and stop—'

I didn't finish that sentence because Dad slapped me in the face. I blinked, amazed by what had just happened. Dad had never hit me before. I stared at him and blinked back a few tears.

'Danny,' he said quietly, stepping back now and looking equally shocked by what he'd done. 'Danny,

I'm sorry—'

I stopped listening. I closed my eyes and said nothing and waited until he left the room. I didn't want to live there any more.

*   *   *

The doorbell rang an hour later and I thought I was imagining things when I heard Sarah's voice downstairs. I ran down and found Dad talking to her.

'Danny, go back to your room, please,' he said in an exhausted voice.

'What's going on?' I asked.

'I came by to say I'm sorry,' said Sarah, who was standing in the hallway now. 'Mam and Dad are going crazy with me too. They think I'm in my room but I climbed out the window.'

'Oh, this just gets better and better,' said Dad, laughing in frustration. 'Sarah, I don't know what to say to you. You really shouldn't be here. If your parents discover that you're missing—'

'They won't care,' she said. 'All they think about is Andy anyway.'

'Because he's in the hospital,' said Dad as he ran a hand across his eyes. 'Of course they're going to spend all their time thinking about him when he's so sick.'

'Can she come upstairs to my room to talk?' I asked.

'No!' snapped Dad. 'Absolutely not!'

'But why not?'

'Because she's supposed to be at home,' he said. 'Her parents will be worried. And she has no reason to be here. You two,' and here he looked from one of us to the other, 'you two have no business being friends. Sarah, I have nothing against you personally, but it does not help what this family is going through having you here. Do you understand that? And it doesn't help your family having Danny coming to visit your brother or hiding under his bed either. Why is that so difficult for you both to understand?'

'I just wanted to talk to him,' said Sarah. 'I wanted to explain.'

'Go home, Sarah,' said Dad.

She considered it and made a move towards the staircase, but he stepped in front of her and shook his head.

'Go home,' he repeated. 'Please. Just do as I ask. If Rachel comes home—'

'Don't go, Sarah,' I pleaded with her.

She looked up at me and shook her head. 'I'm sorry,' she said. 'I better.'

'Thank you,' said Dad quietly.

She turned and headed for the door. 'I'll call you,' I shouted after her. 'I'll be in touch.'

'No you won't,' said Dad.

He closed the door behind her and I turned and ran back to my room.

He called after me but I didn't answer, just locked myself in. I ran over to the window, intending to open it and call out to her on the street. When I got there, however, I saw something that made my stomach turn in jealousy.

Sarah was standing at the end of the driveway, but she wasn't alone. She was speaking to Luke Kennedy, who seemed to be talking very quickly about something. In the middle of whatever he was saying, she shook her head and smiled at him and then he started laughing. My bike was lying in the driveway and he pointed towards it and she shook her head at whatever he had said. Then he must have said something else, because she nodded and he ran back towards his own house where I couldn't see him any more.

I frowned. I wasn't sure what was going on but it didn't seem good. I hated the idea of the two of them talking to each other. I reached for the handle on the window to open it but then Luke came back with his own bike. He put one leg over but didn't sit on the saddle, standing over the crossbar instead with both feet on the ground. Sarah walked towards him and held one of his arms as she climbed on behind him. He wobbled a little at first but then took control of the bike and cycled off down the street, stopping at the end for a moment, before turning right and disappearing out of sight.

I didn't care. I didn't want to see either of them ever again anyway. Or Dad. Or Mam. I glanced at my watch. It was seven o'clock and I could see Mam walking back up the street towards us, a carton of milk in one hand. I made up my mind. I would wait until everyone had gone to bed.

And then I would run away.

*   *   *

I waited until it was very dark, nearly half past eleven, before leaving the house. Mam and Dad were both in bed and I packed a bag with a change of clothes in it, and went down to the kitchen to get some biscuits and a bottle of water to take with me. I wasn't really sure where I was going. I just knew I didn't want to be at home any more. Anyway, I was thirteen years old and figured it was about time I started to make my own way in the world. David Copperfield had started a lot younger than that.

I let myself out the back door and looked down the street to make sure no one was out there. Putting my bag on my back, I jumped on my bike and took off down the main road.

As far as I was concerned, I was never coming home again.

CHAPTER TEN

I didn't sleep at all the first night.

I cycled as far as the school where there was a quiet spot behind the sports hall to hide out. I should have brought a sleeping bag with me but I hadn't thought of it before I left the house, so I tried to sleep without one. Every time I closed my eyes I was afraid that something would come around the corner, a big dog or a tramp perhaps, and kill me.

After a couple of hours I thought about going home again but decided against it. I couldn't give up that easily. In the end I stayed awake all night and only started to nod off when it got bright again. By then it was just after seven o'clock in the morning, and I thought I'd better keep moving or I'd be found.

I'd brought some money with me from home, the ten pounds that Pete had sent me from Amsterdam for my birthday. I parked my bike and went for a burger and chips at a fast-food restaurant. It felt strange eating a burger and chips so early in the morning, but the restaurant was open so I didn't think they'd look at me like I was crazy. When I came out, a bad thing had happened. Someone had stolen my bike. I'd left it on the street and hadn't locked it because I'd forgotten to bring the chain with me from home.

Later that afternoon I started to feel hungry again. I went for another burger and chips and this time I had an ice cream with it, and because it was really good I went back for another one. I only had three pounds left by then but I decided I could make that last for a long time if I put my mind to it. I started to feel nervous walking around the streets in town, especially when I saw any policemen coming my way. I knew that Dad had probably called them and told them that I'd run away and they'd want to find me. I thought it was up to me whether I lived at home or not but I knew they wouldn't agree with me.

Around four o'clock I went in to the shopping centre and up to the cinema on the top floor. They had a special kids' show on around that time and it was exactly £3 to get in. That was what I had left, so I bought a ticket for it because I wanted to sit down somewhere warm and quiet. I was bored with walking around the shops and keeping out of the way of policemen.

I didn't go back to the school that night, because I decided that, when you're on the run, you should change where you go every night so that no one ever finds you. So I walked around town until it was nearly empty and then I went to the car park behind the shopping centre and sat down with my back against the wall. It was a bit close to the big skips where they kept all the rubbish. I was going to move because it smelled so bad, but after a while I didn't notice the smell any more so I stayed where I was. I started to think about my bed at home, and how comfortable it was, and how Mam used to make it every day when I went to school. That made me feel sad but I didn't cry, because you can't cry when you've run away from home and are living off your wits.

I kept thinking about food too because I was so hungry and my stomach was making funny noises. But there was nothing I could do about that since I had no money left and the shops were all closed anyway.

I didn't really sleep that night either, but every so often I'd doze off and then my head would suddenly fall down and I'd wake up again suddenly and feel very cold all over. I hated when that happened so I tried to stay awake but I couldn't, and it kept happening over and over again. The night seemed to last longer than the night before. I tried not to look at my watch too often. Every time I thought that maybe another two or three hours had passed I'd look at it, but it would turn out that only ten or fifteen minutes had gone by.

When it was bright again, I got up and my whole body felt sore. My arms and legs were really stiff and I realized that I hadn't changed my clothes in two days. I wondered what I would do with my day, and decided it was time to go to London and get a job because I couldn't just stay there for ever.

And then I got a surprise, because I was walking past a television shop and I stopped for a minute to look at all the televisions in the window. They all had the same channel on and I suppose it was the news but I couldn't hear anything, just see the pictures. A photograph came up on the screen of a boy and I thought he looked a bit like me. It took me a few seconds to realize that it *was* me and, when I did, my stomach went all funny inside and then the photograph went off the screen again. It was replaced by a reporter who was standing outside my house, and I thought I'd better move away from there quickly before anyone noticed that they had a celebrity in their midst. But everyone was going to work, I suppose, and no one even looked at me as I made my way down the street.

That was when I knew I was totally on my own.

A few hours later, I started to worry about the fact that I was really hungry and my arms and legs were beginning to feel like jelly. Also, I hadn't slept in two and a half days so I was feeling dizzy too. I thought about going home but I knew that, if I did, I'd never be let out of the house again until I was thirty, so it didn't seem like a good idea. I wasn't sure what Mam or Dad would do to me if they caught up with me. There was nothing I wanted to do more than go home and have some food and take a bath and sit down in front of the television with both of them.

Because I'd seen myself on the news, I knew that everyone would be looking for me and I thought it would be best if I got a disguise, so I went in to a clothes shop and stole a woollen hat. I'd never stolen anything in my life before. It was easier than I imagined. I just walked in to the biggest clothes shop I could find, took a hat off a rack, ripped the tag off, put it on my head and left. I felt a bit scared leaving the shop, but no one came after me so I started to run just to be safe. I was too tired and hungry to run for long and it made me feel even dizzier than before, so I stopped. I caught sight of myself in a mirror then and I looked funny wearing the hat because it was such a hot day, but I didn't think anyone would recognize me in it so I kept it on.

When I looked at my watch it was just after one o'clock and the streets were busy with people buying sandwiches and going to lunch. Every time I saw someone eating something on the street I felt my mouth start to water and my stomach begin to hurt. It wasn't making funny sounds any more, it was just hurting me.

I wanted to go to London then but wasn't sure how to get there. I didn't have any money to buy a ticket for the train or the bus, and I was afraid that there would be policemen at the stations looking out for me. I wished I still had my bike because then I could have cycled there, even though it might have taken weeks. But that would have been part of the adventure and I wouldn't have minded. I started to think that I might have to walk instead. And although that seemed like a stupid idea, I remembered that David Copperfield had walked all the way from London to Dover on his own and that, if he could do it, then so could I.

I fell asleep that night between some trees at the end of the rugby field at school. I should have thought of going there before, because the ground was much softer than at the sports hall or the car park, and it didn't make my back feel so sore. I put my bag under my head for a pillow and used my coat as a blanket and managed to fall asleep for a few hours. When I woke up, though, I felt worse than ever. For a few minutes I didn't even know who I was or why I was out in the open air, and, when I remembered, I wondered whether things would ever change. Even though it had only been three days since I'd been at home, it felt like three years, three lifetimes. I wondered whether Dad and Mam had got used to not having me around any more.

When I stood up, though, something bad happened. I fell over. I stood up again, and this time I had to put my arms out by my sides as if I was walking along a tightrope. It took a few minutes for me to feel steady. Once I did, my stomach started hurting again and I found myself doubling over in agony. I looked around, wondering whether there was anything I could eat. But then I realized that I didn't want to eat any more, even though I hadn't had anything since the second burger the afternoon of the first day. I didn't really feel hungry, just in pain.

That day went by in a blur of walking the streets and wanting to eat. Sometimes I felt like going home but I knew that I couldn't.

I was running out of places to stay but I hadn't been to the park yet, so I decided I'd sleep there that night. It wasn't very far away either, which was good because I knew I wasn't going to be able to walk for much longer. My legs were too shaky underneath me.

I got to the park around midnight and it was empty. I walked past the bench where I had sat with Sarah and it made me sad to remember it. I hadn't realized then how lucky I was to have a home to go back to, and food in the fridge, and a mam and dad, even if one of them wasn't speaking to anyone and the other one had hit me. It was still better than living like this. I wanted to go home then but it was too late, because I didn't think they'd ever let me in now after what I'd done.

I found a quiet spot near some bushes and put my bag under my head like I'd done the night before, but, just as I was about to lie down on the ground, I fell instead and hit my arm against a tree. I tried to stand up but couldn't because my legs weren't working any more. When I looked at my arm it had started to bleed, but it didn't feel sore, and the more I looked at it, the more dizzy I got. I looked around at the trees and the bushes and the park, and all the colours seemed to get blurry until I didn't know where I was. It felt a bit like the park was getting smaller and smaller and smaller and crowding in on me, and when it did it would suffocate me and that would be that. I'd just be dead, or maybe in a coma like that boy whose name I couldn't remember any more. So I tried to open my eyes wider, to make all the blurriness stop. But when I did that it just made my stomach hurt even more.

I cried out and bent over to stop it hurting so much, and I thought that if I could just stand up then I'd feel better. But every time I tried to get to my feet, my legs wouldn't work right and I'd just fall over again. The last time I tried, I fell even harder and landed on my back and I lay there, staring up at the sky, and decided that I wasn't going to get up ever again. I was just going to lie there and not move until they found me. I wondered whether I was going to die.

I started to close my eyes and everything got dark, but just when I did that, just when I closed my eyes, I felt something strange happening. It was like there was someone standing over me, saying my name, but I didn't know who it was so I thought I was just imagining things.

Then the figure leaned down and I felt his arms going underneath me and picking me up, and I was lifted off the ground, and nothing hurt any more because I couldn't feel anything. I thought this was what it must feel like to die, that this was the moment of my death, but I wasn't sure if it really was. I tried as hard as I could to open my eyes one last time to see who it was, to know who had found me, who was carrying me across the park, who had saved my life. When I did, when I opened them, I knew who it was. I wanted to talk to him but my voice wasn't working any more. I could only say one word and it came out like a croak and didn't sound like me at all. After I said it, I closed my eyes and everything went black.

'Pete,' I said.

CHAPTER ELEVEN

And then one morning, out of the blue, Andy woke up.

A nurse went in to his hospital room to check on him and he was lying there, eyes open, wide awake, wondering where he was and what he was doing there and asking for his mam and dad. We were eating breakfast in the kitchen when the phone rang. Dad took the call, and when he came back in to the room he looked very pale and none of us knew what had happened. He walked over to Mam, who might have thought the worst, but he put his arms around her instead and told her that everything was going to be all right. That Andy was awake again. That he wasn't in a coma any more. That he wasn't going to die. She started crying then, but it wasn't like the crying she had done throughout the rest of the summer. She was crying because it was all over and Andy was going to get better after all.

That was the first morning after I got home from the hospital. I'd been brought there after Pete found me in the park, and I'd had to stay in for six nights because the doctor said I had been in danger of catching pneumonia and I was dehydrated too. I don't remember much about those few days, except that when I woke up in the hospital bed I was starving. They only gave me small things to eat though, because they said they didn't want to shock my system. And they were all there watching over me: Pete, Dad and even Mam. The whole family was back together.

At home, I was supposed to stay in bed all day until I got my strength back. That was what the doctors had said anyway. So I was back in my room a couple of hours later when there was a knock on my door and Pete walked in, closing it behind him.

'Heard the news?' he asked, a wide smile on his face.

'Yes,' I replied. It had gone lunchtime by then and he'd only just got out of bed. His hair was all over the place and he needed a shave.

'So how are you feeling now?' he asked me.

'I'm all right,' I said. 'A bit tired. I keep falling asleep. And I'm still hungry even though I keep eating.'

'You'll get back to normal soon enough,' he said. 'You gave us all quite a fright, you know. Mam and Dad were going nuts.'

I nodded and looked away. I felt a bit ashamed of myself, especially because no one seemed to be angry with me for running away in the first place. Instead, they had been nicer to me than they had ever been before.

'When did you get here?' I asked him then. 'I thought you were in Europe.'

'I was in Europe,' he said. 'I was in Prague and Dad phoned me and told me you'd gone missing.'

'And you came back?'

He sat back and looked surprised. 'Of course I came back,' he said. 'What do you think? I came back immediately. I was here within about six hours of that phone call. Everyone was looking for you. You were gone for three days, Danny,' he said then, looking quite serious. 'What did you do anyway?'

'I just walked around,' I told him. 'I ate burgers on the first day and wandered around the shops. And then I tried to sleep in different places, but it wasn't easy because I was outside. By the time I got to the park that night I hadn't eaten in ages and I didn't feel well and I thought I was going to die. But you found me.'

He smiled a little but looked sad too. 'You shouldn't have done it, Danny. You know that, don't you? You shouldn't have just run away like that.'

'I had to,' I said. 'You don't know what it was like. You weren't here. Mam wouldn't speak to anyone and she was walking around in a daze all the time. And Dad had to do all the things in the house and he wasn't good at any of them. Then he got angry with me because I'd made friends with Andy's sister—'

'Yeah, I heard about that too,' said Pete, shaking his head. 'That wasn't very smart.'

'Why wasn't it?' I asked. 'What was wrong with it?'

'Because you spent all your time running around after her, making sure she was all right, when you should have been taking care of Mam instead. That's what we're here for.'

'But she wasn't talking to me,' I protested. 'You weren't here, Pete. You don't know.'

'I know I wasn't here, but—'

'And I bet you're not even going to

stay now,' I added.

Pete sighed. 'Well, the summer's nearly over,' he told me. 'I have to go back to university in a few weeks.'

I felt myself starting to get upset with him, as if none of this would ever have happened if he'd been there in the first place. 'But you said you weren't going to go to university far away,' I said. 'You told me that last year. And then you changed your mind and went to Scotland when you said you'd stay here with me.'

'Danny, I needed a change—'

'But you promised me!'

'I didn't promise you anything,' he said, keeping calm even though I was getting more and more upset. 'But I'll promise that you can come on a visit if you promise me something.'

'OK,' I said. 'What?'

'That you never do anything as stupid as this ever again. That if you ever feel like running away from home, you call me and talk to me instead, all right?'

'All right,' I said, nodding. 'I promise.'

'Good,' he said, standing up and tousling my hair. 'Then I promise too. Now, I better get a shower. I feel like death.'

'Thanks for saving me,' I said and he turned and smiled at me.

'What are big brothers for?' he asked.

*   *   *

We went to stay with Gran and Granddad for a few days before school started again. Pete didn't come with us because he said he could still go to Vienna and Berlin if he got his skates on, so Mam asked Luke Kennedy whether he'd like to come with us instead. It turned out that, when he'd cycled off with Sarah that day, he'd gone with her to tell her parents that I wasn't as horrible as they thought I was. Their meeting didn't end very well either, I don't think. Although it wasn't long after that the three of us became friends. Which led to other problems later, but that's another story.

'You're looking a lot better, young man,' Benjamin Benson told me as I walked towards the car. 'Gave us all quite a scare though.'

'Now that's all in the past,' said Mrs Kennedy. 'You've had a difficult summer, Danny, haven't you?'

'I suppose,' I said, putting my bag in the car. 'Thanks for letting Luke come with us.'

'Letting him?' she said, laughing. 'Good Lord, Danny, I never would have heard the end of it if I'd said no. Between you and me he hasn't had a very good summer either. He was supposed to spend a lot of it with his father but . . .' She shrugged and stood back again, shaking her head, and Mr Benson put an arm around her waist. 'Oh, here he is now,' she said then, as Luke came out of my house with Mam, carrying one of her bags for her.

'Isn't he a perfect gentleman?' asked Mam, smiling for the first time in ages. She'd been to the hairdresser's the day before too, and was starting to look more like her old self. She was wearing a new pair of jeans and a white top, and she looked like she couldn't wait to have a few days away. 'He came in and offered to help me with my bags. You have him well trained, Alice.'

Mrs Kennedy laughed. 'He's not like that at home,' she said.

'Yes I am,' grunted Luke, putting the bag in the boot of the car.

Over the next few days we spent most of our time walking around the fields near Gran and Granddad's house. That was when Luke told me that he hadn't seen his dad since just before Christmas, and that every time Luke called him on the phone he always sounded happy to hear from him at first, but then he only stayed on for a few minutes before saying he had to go. And that every time his dad said that Luke could come and stay with him, he always found a reason to cancel just before he went. So Luke had decided not to ask any more because it made him too sad when it happened.

'Benjamin,' he said to me one afternoon when we were walking around the farm, looking for rabbits. 'He's not so bad really, is he?'

'I like him,' I said. 'He's funny.'

'He's kind of stupid.'

'Well yes,' I admitted. 'Kind of. But he's funny too.'

Luke nodded. 'He gave me twenty pounds when I was leaving,' he told me. 'And he said I wasn't to tell Mam and I was to spend it all on sweets and things that weren't good for me. And he said that, when I went back to school and the new season started, he'd take me to some matches if I wanted to go.'

'And what did you say?'

He shrugged his shoulders. 'I said I

114

wouldn't mind,' he told me, and I knew that meant he was going to go.

* * *

On the last night of the school holidays, just after I'd gone to bed, Mam knocked on my bedroom door and came in to see me.

'Can I come in?' she asked and I nodded. I moved over in the bed so she could sit down. When she did, she stared at me for a few moments as if she was trying to understand something. Then she smiled at me and shook her head.

'All set for tomorrow?' she asked.

'I think so,' I said.

'That's good. I'm sorry you didn't have much of a summer holiday.'

'It doesn't matter,' I said.

'It does matter, Danny,' she said. 'It was such a horrible time. I know that no one will ever understand what I was going through, what it felt like to be responsible for something

115

like that, but just the idea of hurting that boy . . . If he hadn't got better, I don't know how I would have coped with it. To be honest, I can't see myself ever getting behind the wheel of a car again.'

'But it wasn't your fault,' I told her.

'I know, I know,' she said, smiling. 'But it doesn't matter about that. I don't think I'd feel confident. Look at all the people it affected. And look at what I did to you.'

'But you didn't do anything to me,' I said, because I didn't like the idea of Mam saying sorry to me for something. It was me who was usually saying sorry to her for things.

'I did,' she said. 'I let you down. I wasn't your mam for the last few weeks, and look where that led you. Anything could have happened to you when you were on your own out there. Don't ever do that to me again, do you hear me?' she added fiercely and I nodded.

'I won't,' I said.

'Well,' she said. 'It's all behind us now. You're back to school tomorrow. Andy Maclean is back home with his family. Everything is as it should be again. From tomorrow morning, we all get back to normal, all right?'

I smiled and nodded. That was what I wanted to hear. She reached forward and gave me a kiss before standing up and heading over towards the door. 'Don't stay up too late,' she said before leaving. 'You've got school in the morning.'

'I won't,' I said.

She left the room and I sat there for a few moments. I felt as if all the problems of the last few weeks had finally slipped away and that my old life, the one I thought was gone for ever, would come back to me from the moment I woke up the next morning. I reached over to my bedside table and took *David Copperfield* off the shelf. I hadn't read it in ages, but it was time to go back to it now because I'd wasted all that time during the summer, when I could have got to the end of it and started another one.

My bookmark was still there, halfway through, and I started reading. It was the bit where David goes to see Agnes after he gets drunk at the theatre the night before, and she says it doesn't matter, that she forgives him, and he tells her that she's his good angel.